To my sisters, who are also my best friends,

Jill Swistak, Gina Schneider, and Linda Mammano

With special thanks to California Board Shop and James Adkins

Book design by Lucy Nielsen. Typeset in Gill Sans.

Printed in Hong Kong.

Library of Congress Cataloging-in-Publication Data

Mammano, Julie.

Rhinos who snowboard / by Julie Mammano

p. cm.

Summary: Snowboarding rhinos check out the weather,
head for the slopes, and spend all day out on
the snow-covered mountains.

Includes a glossary of snowboarding lingo.

ISBN: 0-8118-1715-6

[1. Snowboarding—Fiction. 2. Rhinoceroses—Fiction.] I. Title

PZ7.M3117Rf 1997

[E]—dc21   97-1349   CIP

AC

Distributed in Canada by Raincoast Books

8680 Cambie Street

Vancouver, B.C. V6P 6M9

10 9 8 7 6 5 4 3 2 1

Chronicle Books, 85 Second Street

San Francisco, California 94105

website: www.chronbooks.com

JULIE MAMMANO

Rhinos Who Snowboard

chronicle books · san francisco

They load up their gear and head for the slopes.

They strap on their boards and take a lift to the GNARLIEST peaks.

They reach the top and . . .

JUMP!

They BUST OUT fast down the FALL LINE!

They go **TOTALLY AGGRO.**

They **CHARGE** the steepest slopes.

They ride through the backcountry.

They carve perfect POWDER FANS.

Rhinos who snowboard FLOAT STIFFY TAILGRABS.

They catch PHAT AIR over INSANE GAPS.

They plant HOHOS off the lip of a windblown HALFPIPE.

Rhinos who snowboard are SPIN MASTERS.

They **LAUNCH MAJOR** backflips.

It is so UNCOOL when MOGUL hopping KOOKS botch up their big jumps.

At the end of the day, they take their final run.

They are **STOKED TO THE MAX.**

Last one down is a **POSER.**

Rhinos who snowboard CHILL OUT while loads of PHAT POW DUMP outside.

Tomorrow will be
EPIC!

Board Speak

air jump trick

bonk to hit an object on purpose for style

bummer really bad

bust out to start quickly then go fast

charge go for it

chill out relax

dump to snowfall in big amounts

epic really great

faceplant to land on your face

fakie to ride backwards

fall line straight down a slope of a mountain

float to make a big jump

freefall to fall airborne straight down

gnarliest biggest, scariest

halfpipe curve in snow shaped like a tube

hohos two handed handstands

huck to jump wildly

insane gaps big spaces between cliffs or slopes

kooks jerks who ski or snowboard

pow powdery snow

powder fans snow sprayed in the shape of a fan

rude really bad

slams crashes

spin master one who does spin tricks

stiffy with both legs straight

stoked to the max really happy

tailgrabs grab the back of the board

totally aggro fearless

uncool bad

launch to take off on a jump

major very

mogul bump in the snow

phat really big, high, or great

poser pretend snowboarder

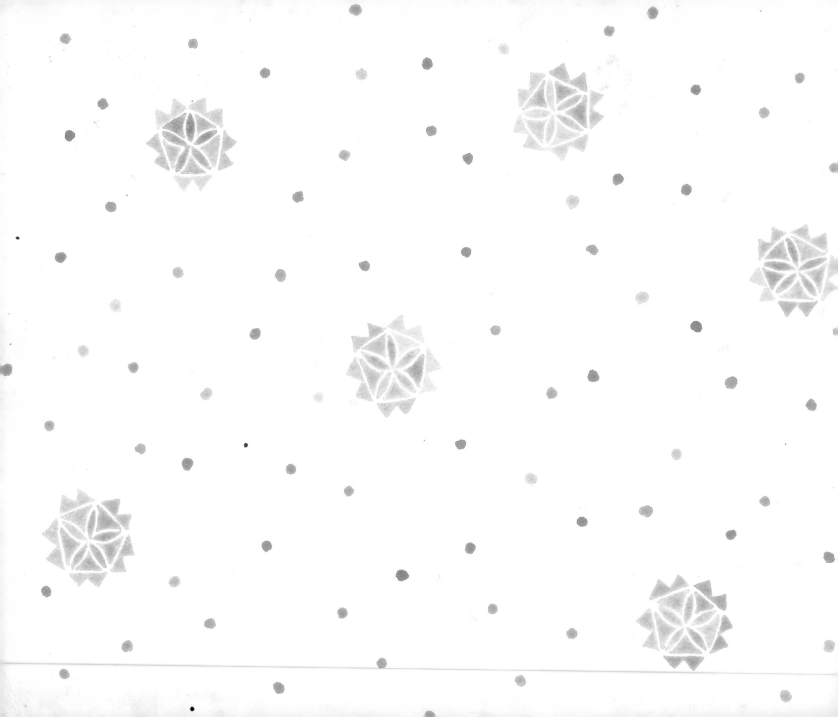